D1415353

STONE ARCH BOOKS
a capstone imprint

W STONE ARCH BOOKS™

Published in 2014
A Capstone Imprint
1710 Roe Crest Drive
North Mankato, MN 56003
www.capstonepub.com

Originally published by DC Comics in the U.S. in
single magazine form as The Batman Strikes! #4.
Copyright © 2014 DC Comics. All Rights Reserved.

DC Comics
1700 Broadway, New York, NY 10019
A Warner Bros. Entertainment Company

Printed in China by Nordica.
1013/CA21301918
092013   007744NORD514

Cataloging-in-Publication Data is available at the
Library of Congress website:
ISBN: 978-1-4342-4788-9 (library binding)

Summary: The young Dark Knight faces a foe who
is twice his size and has the wiles of ten men: the
mighty Bane!

STONE ARCH BOOKS
Ashley C. Andersen Zantop *Publisher*
Michael Dahl *Editorial Director*
Sean Tulien *Editor*
Heather Kindseth *Creative Director*
Bob Lentz *Designer*
Kathy McColley *Production Specialist*

DC COMICS
Joan Hilty & Harvey Richards *Original U.S. Editors*
Jeff Matsuda & Dave McCaig *Cover Artists*

BANE ON A RAMPAGE!

BILL MATHENY ....WRITER
CHRISTOPHER JONES ....PENCILLER
TERRY BEATTY...INKER
HEROIC AGE..COLORIST
JARED K. FLETCHER...............................LETTERER

BATMAN CREATED BY
BOB KANE

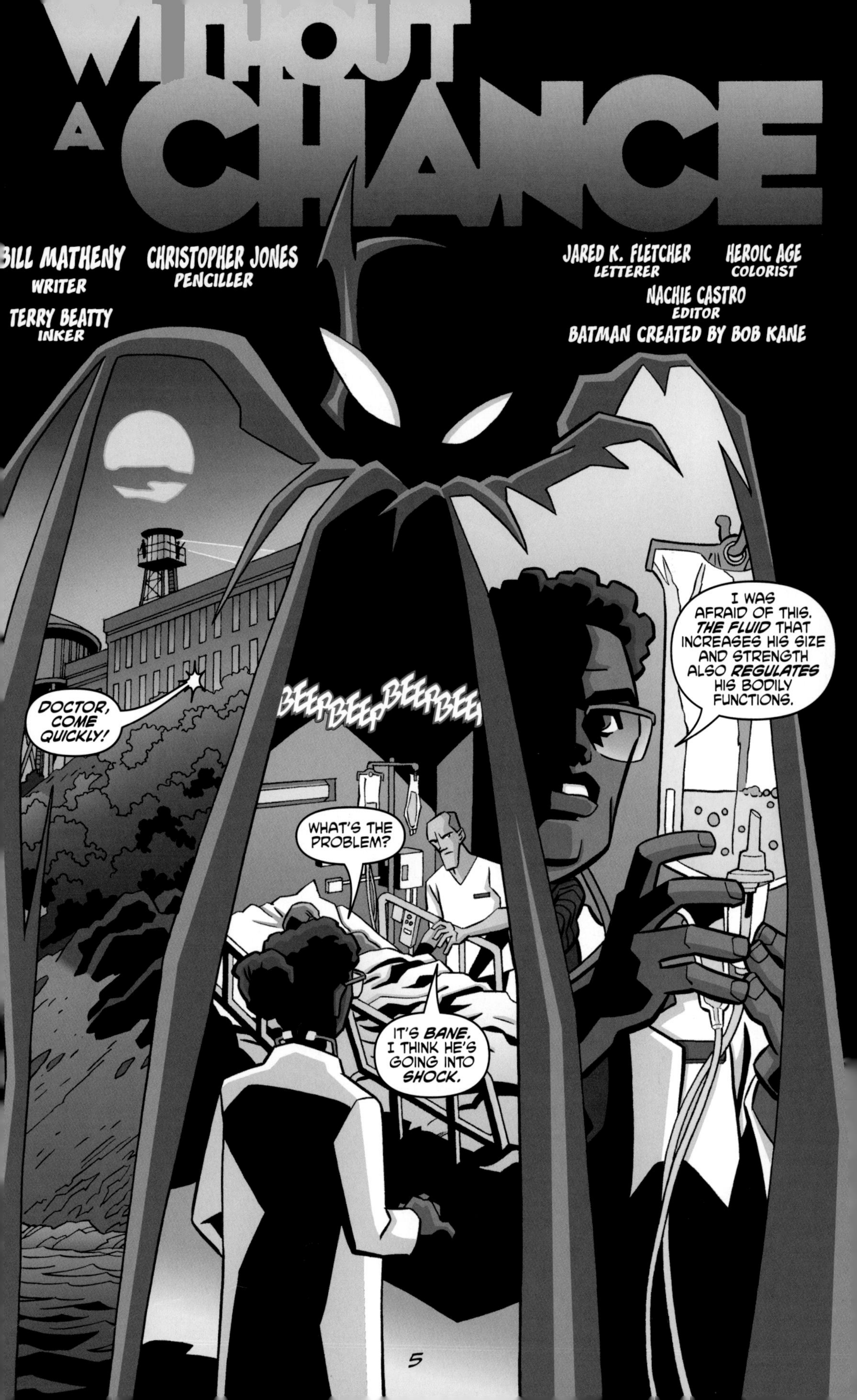
WITHOUT A CHANCE
BILL MATHENY WRITER
CHRISTOPHER JONES PENCILLER
TERRY BEATTY INKER
JARED K. FLETCHER LETTERER
HEROIC AGE COLORIST
NACHIE CASTRO EDITOR
BATMAN CREATED BY BOB KANE
DOCTOR, COME QUICKLY!
BEEP BEEP BEEP BEEP
WHAT'S THE PROBLEM?
IT'S BANE. I THINK HE'S GOING INTO SHOCK.
I WAS AFRAID OF THIS. THE FLUID THAT INCREASES HIS SIZE AND STRENGTH ALSO REGULATES HIS BODILY FUNCTIONS.

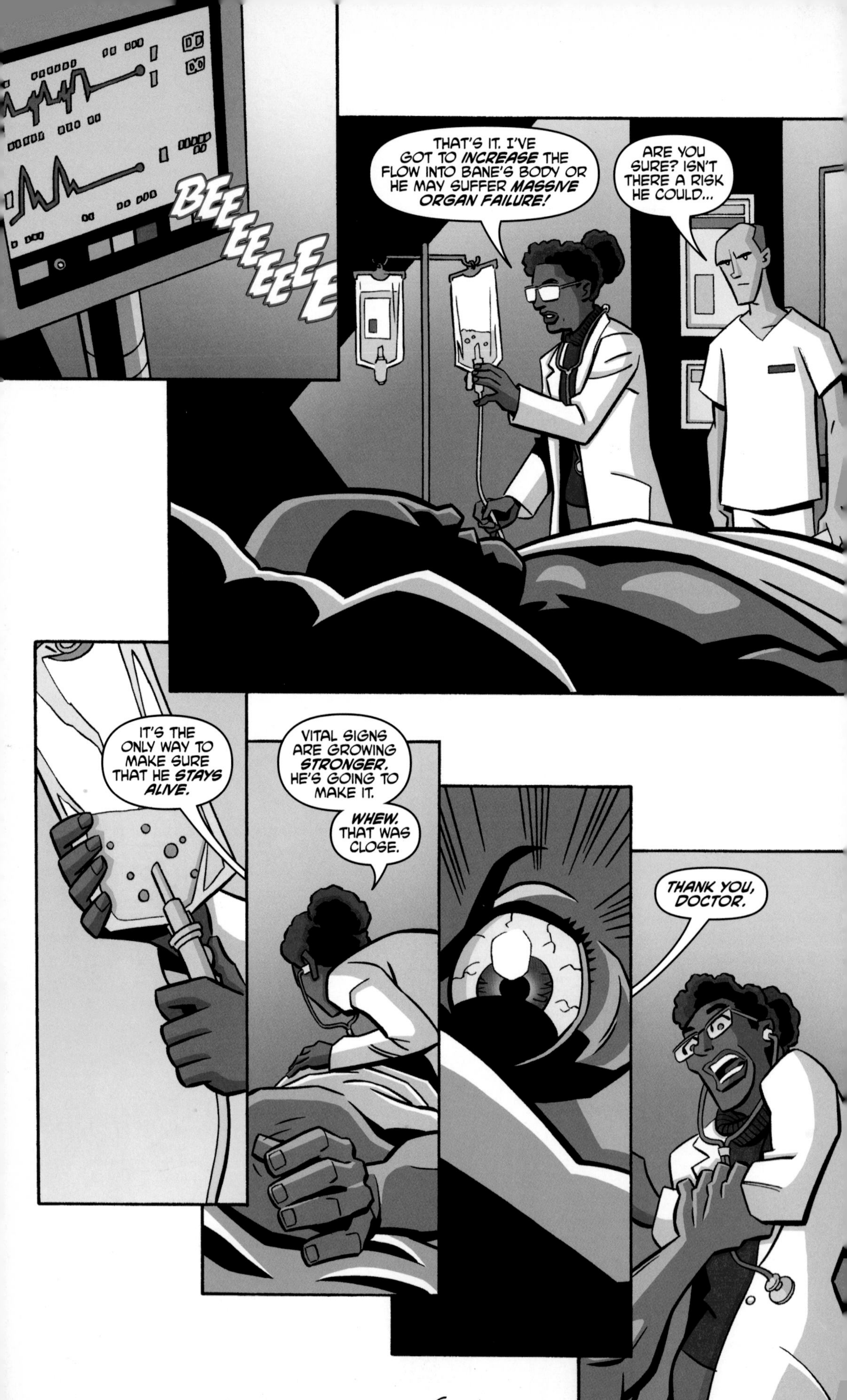
BEEEEEEEE
THAT'S IT. I'VE GOT TO INCREASE THE FLOW INTO BANE'S BODY OR HE MAY SUFFER MASSIVE ORGAN FAILURE!
ARE YOU SURE? ISN'T THERE A RISK HE COULD...
IT'S THE ONLY WAY TO MAKE SURE THAT HE STAYS ALIVE.
VITAL SIGNS ARE GROWING STRONGER. HE'S GOING TO MAKE IT.
WHEW. THAT WAS CLOSE.
THANK YOU, DOCTOR.

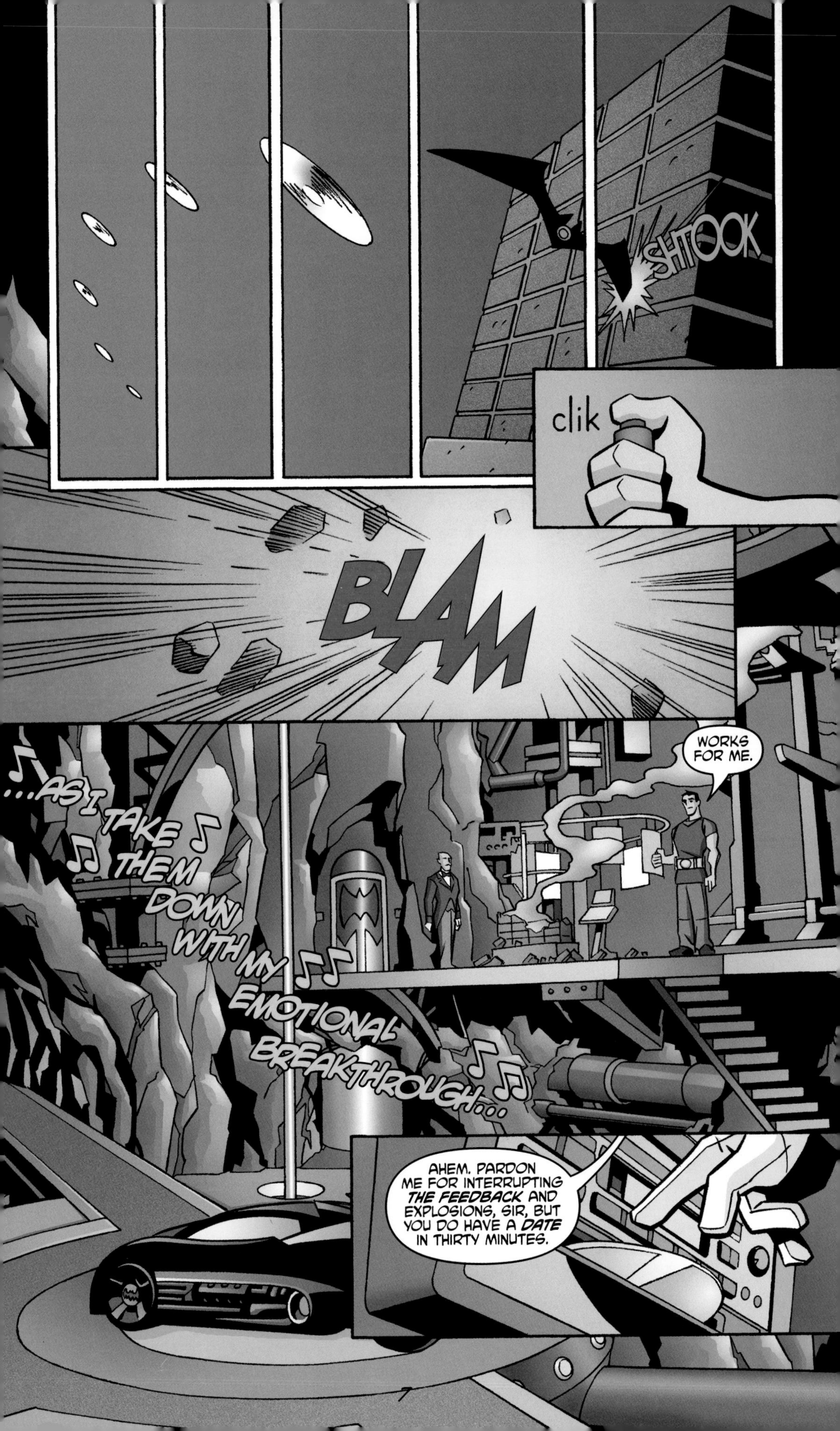
SHTOOK
clik
BLAM
♫ ...AS I TAKE ♫ ♫ THEM DOWN WITH MY ♫♫ EMOTIONAL BREAKTHROUGH... ♫♫
WORKS FOR ME.
AHEM. PARDON ME FOR INTERRUPTING *THE FEEDBACK* AND EXPLOSIONS, SIR, BUT YOU DO HAVE A *DATE* IN THIRTY MINUTES.

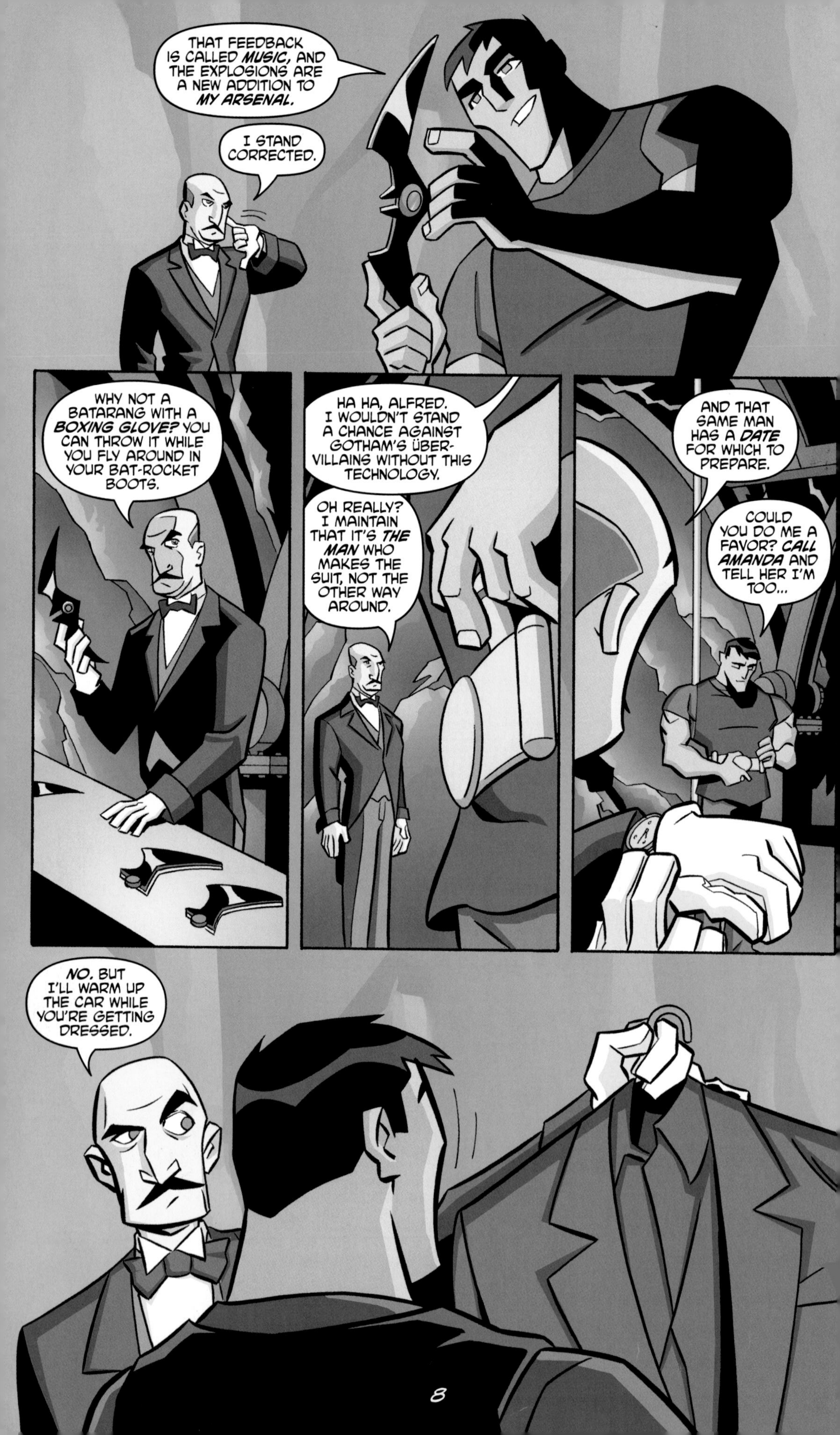
THAT FEEDBACK IS CALLED *MUSIC,* AND THE EXPLOSIONS ARE A NEW ADDITION TO *MY ARSENAL.*
I STAND CORRECTED.
WHY NOT A BATARANG WITH A *BOXING GLOVE?* YOU CAN THROW IT WHILE YOU FLY AROUND IN YOUR BAT-ROCKET BOOTS.
HA HA, ALFRED. I WOULDN'T STAND A CHANCE AGAINST GOTHAM'S ÜBER-VILLAINS WITHOUT THIS TECHNOLOGY.
OH REALLY? I MAINTAIN THAT IT'S *THE MAN* WHO MAKES THE SUIT, NOT THE OTHER WAY AROUND.
AND THAT SAME MAN HAS A *DATE* FOR WHICH TO PREPARE.
COULD YOU DO ME A FAVOR? *CALL AMANDA* AND TELL HER I'M TOO...
NO. BUT I'LL WARM UP THE CAR WHILE YOU'RE GETTING DRESSED.

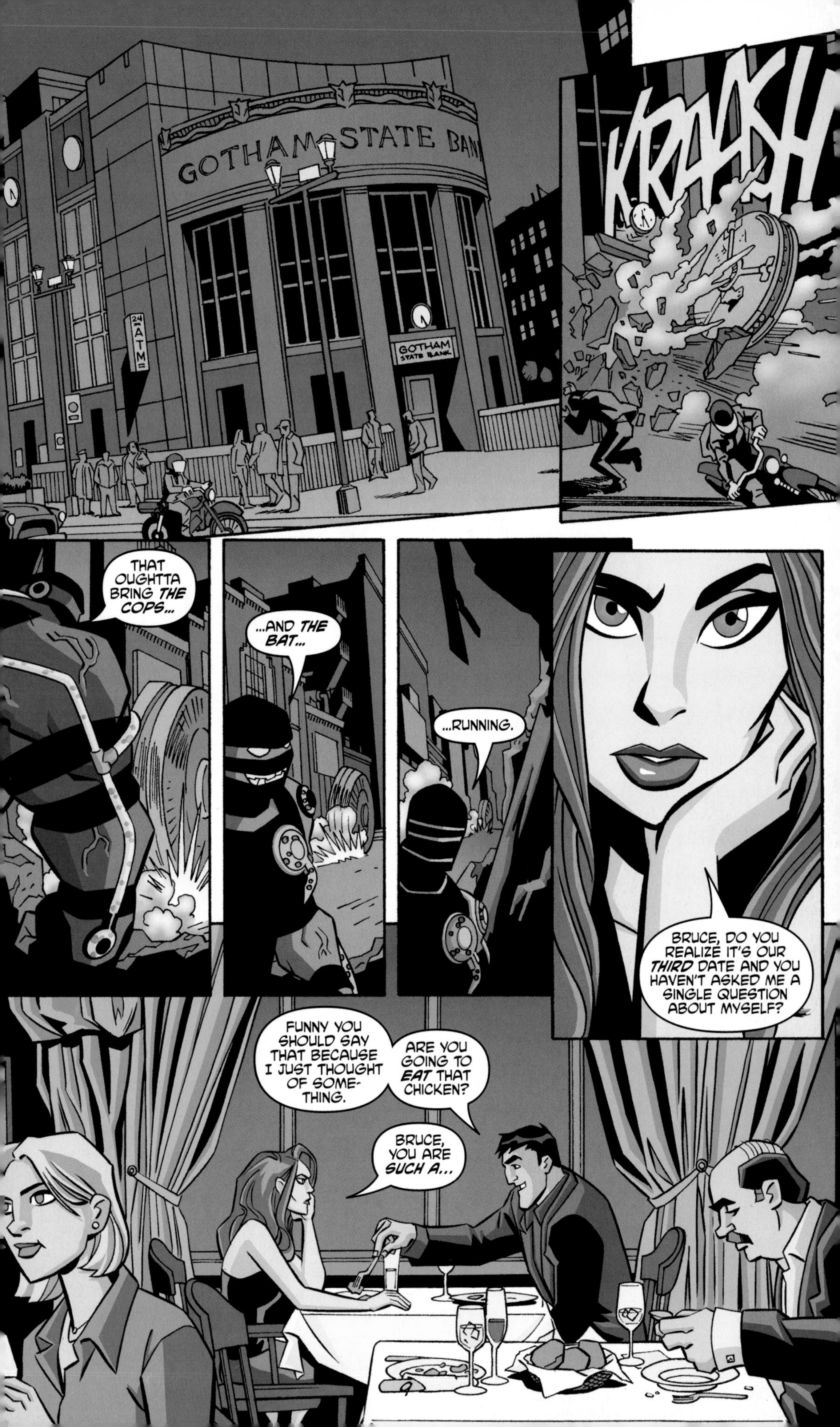
GOTHAM STATE BANK
24 ATM
GOTHAM STATE BANK
KRASH!
THAT OUGHTTA BRING *THE COPS*...
...AND *THE BAT*...
...RUNNING.
BRUCE, DO YOU REALIZE IT'S OUR *THIRD* DATE AND YOU HAVEN'T ASKED ME A SINGLE QUESTION ABOUT MYSELF?
FUNNY YOU SHOULD SAY THAT BECAUSE I JUST THOUGHT OF SOME-THING.
ARE YOU GOING TO *EAT* THAT CHICKEN?
BRUCE, YOU ARE *SUCH A...*

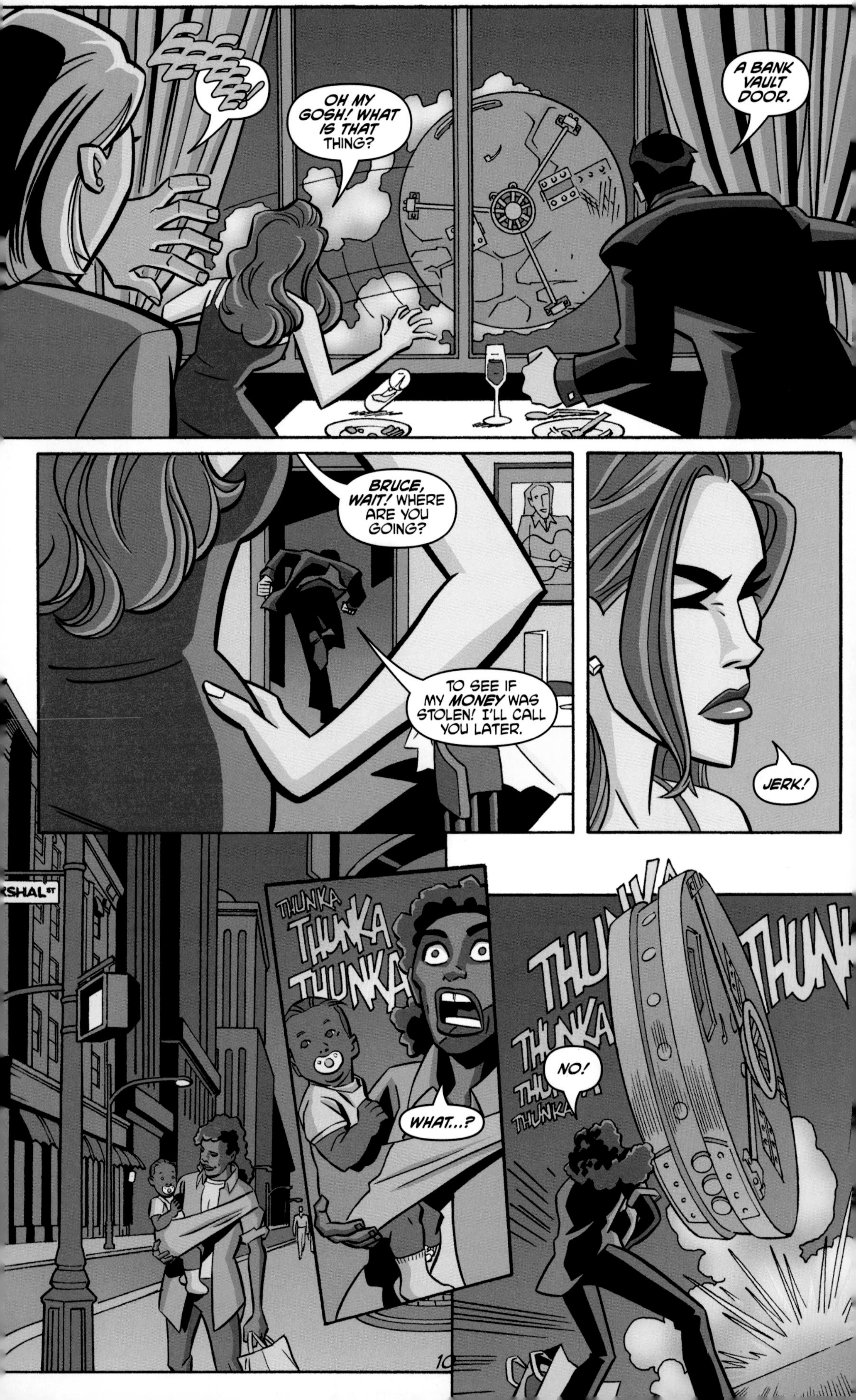

OH MY GOSH! WHAT IS THAT THING?
A BANK VAULT DOOR.
BRUCE, WAIT! WHERE ARE YOU GOING?
TO SEE IF MY MONEY WAS STOLEN! I'LL CALL YOU LATER.
JERK!
RSHAL ST
THUNKA THUNKA THUNKA
WHAT...?
THUNKA THUNKA THUNKA THUNKA THUNKA
NO!

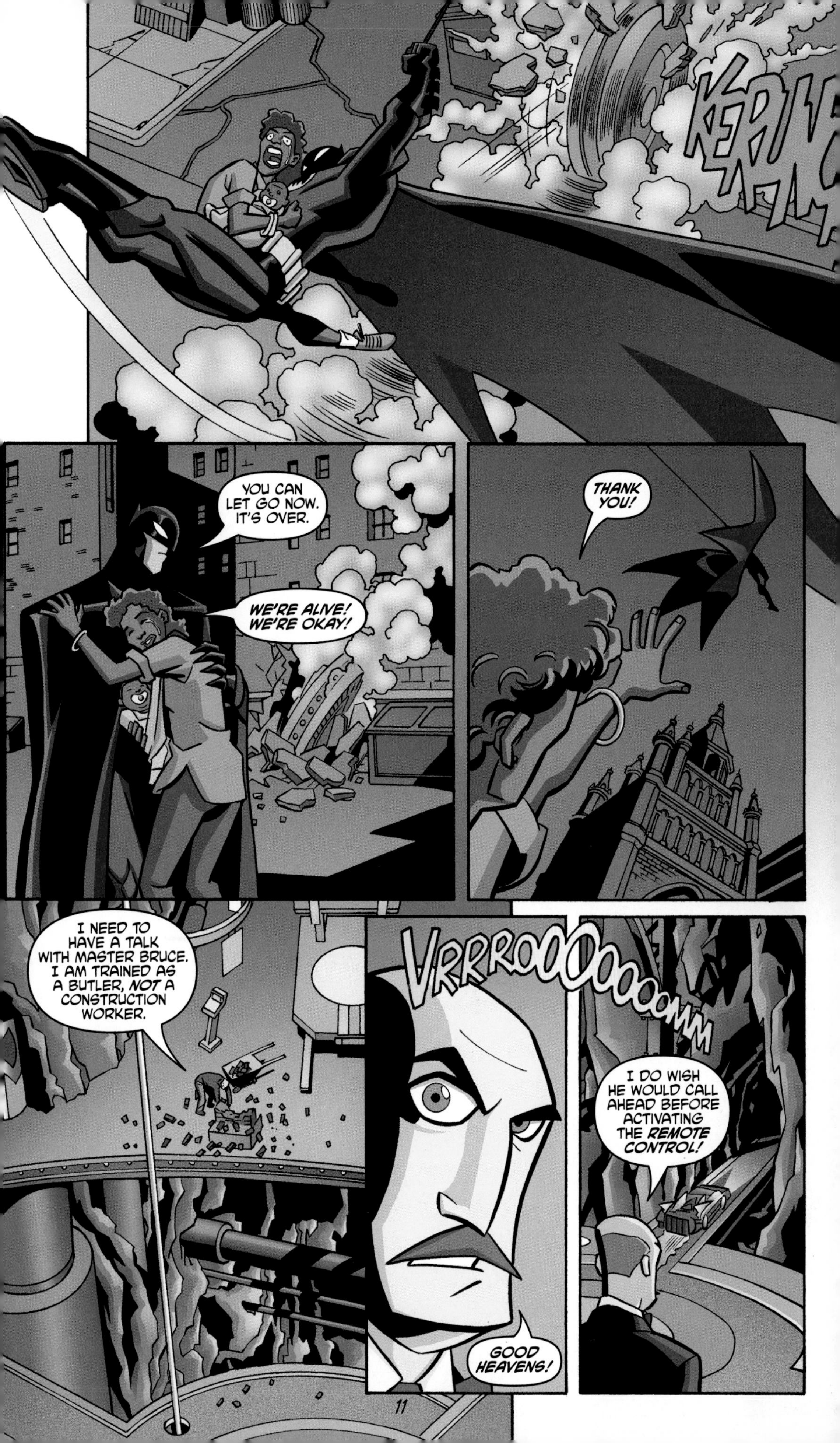
KERWAM
YOU CAN LET GO NOW. IT'S OVER.
WE'RE ALIVE! WE'RE OKAY!
THANK YOU!
I NEED TO HAVE A TALK WITH MASTER BRUCE. I AM TRAINED AS A BUTLER, *NOT* A CONSTRUCTION WORKER.
VRRROOOOOOOOMM
GOOD HEAVENS!
I DO WISH HE WOULD CALL AHEAD BEFORE ACTIVATING THE *REMOTE CONTROL!*

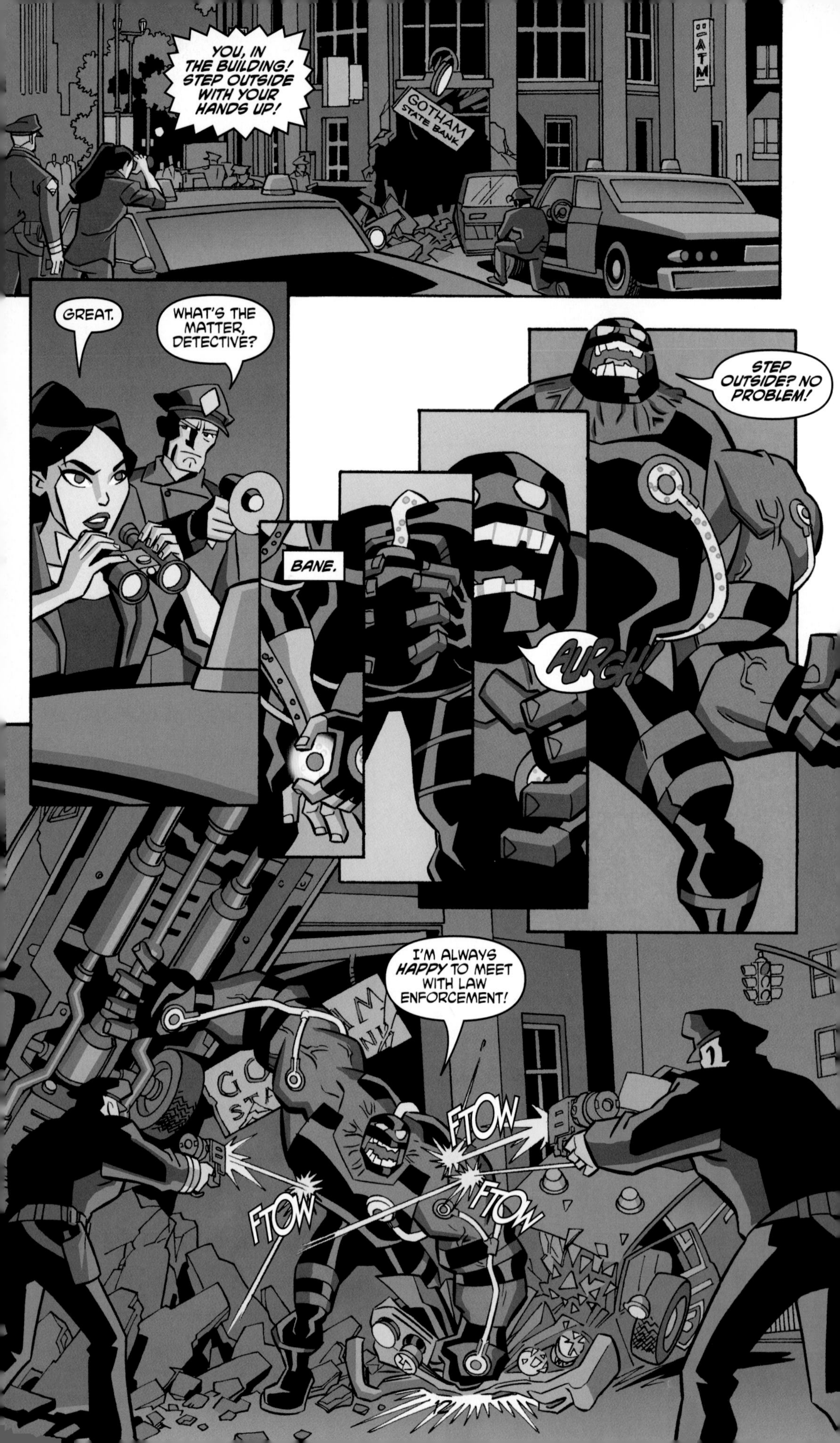
YOU, IN THE BUILDING! STEP OUTSIDE WITH YOUR HANDS UP!
GOTHAM STATE BANK
ATM
GREAT.
WHAT'S THE MATTER, DETECTIVE?
BANE.
STEP OUTSIDE? NO PROBLEM!
AURGH!
I'M ALWAYS HAPPY TO MEET WITH LAW ENFORCEMENT!
FTOW
FTOW
FTOW

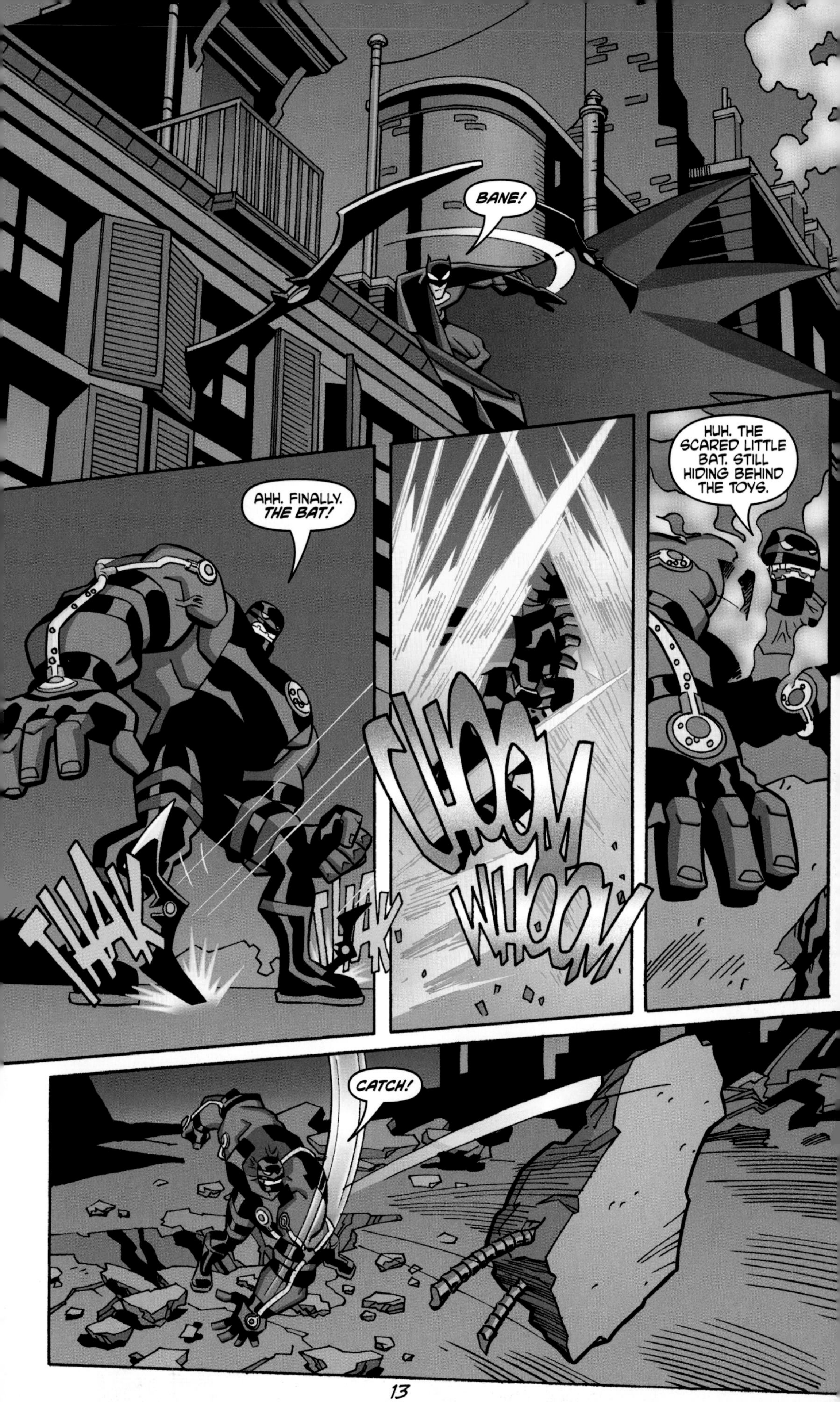
BANE!
AHH. FINALLY. THE BAT!
THAK
THAK
CHOOM
WHOOM
HUH. THE SCARED LITTLE BAT. STILL HIDING BEHIND THE TOYS.
CATCH!

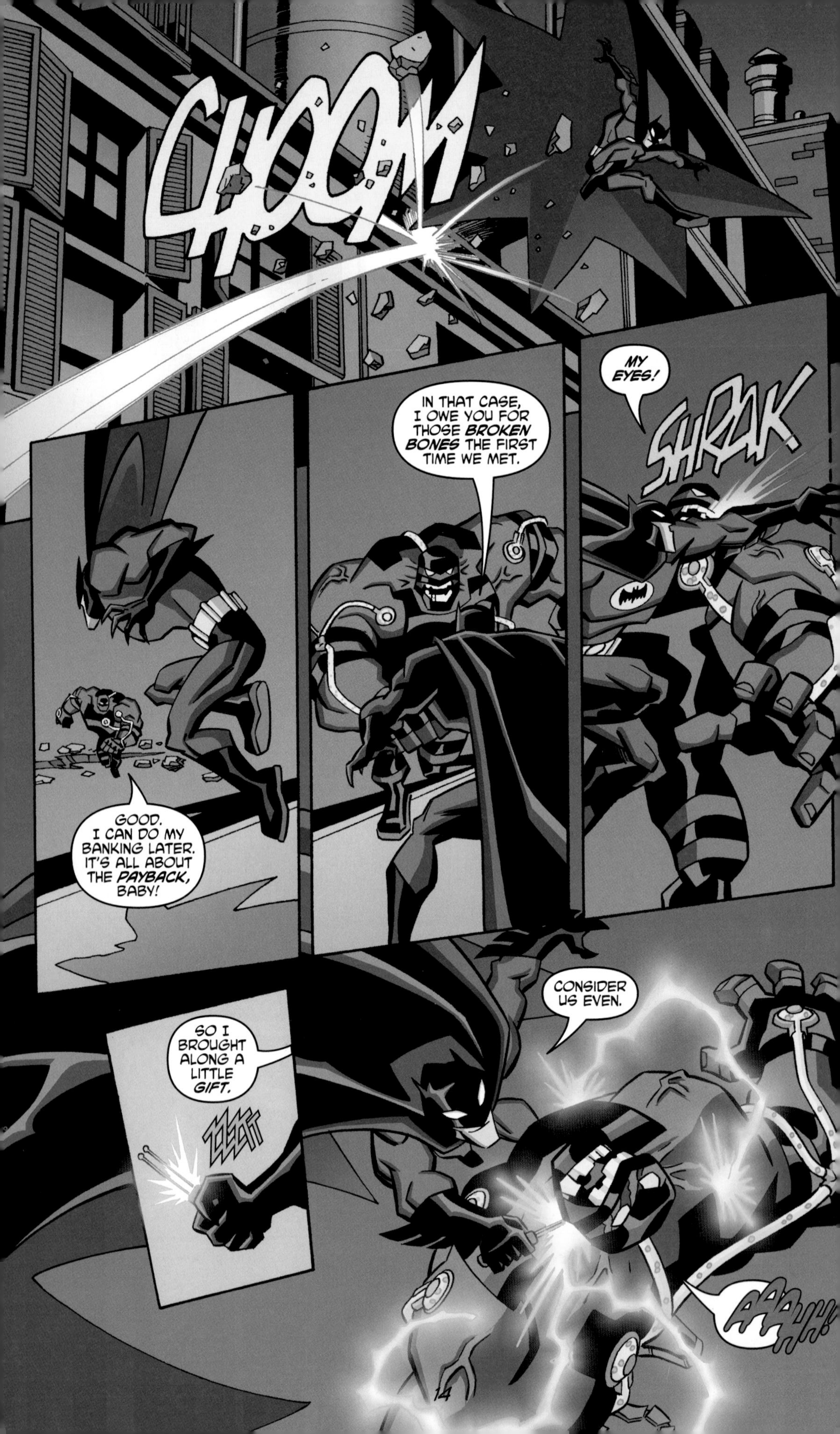
CHOOM
GOOD. I CAN DO MY BANKING LATER. IT'S ALL ABOUT THE PAYBACK, BABY!
IN THAT CASE, I OWE YOU FOR THOSE BROKEN BONES THE FIRST TIME WE MET.
MY EYES!
SHRAK
SO I BROUGHT ALONG A LITTLE GIFT.
ZZZZT
CONSIDER US EVEN.
AAAHH!

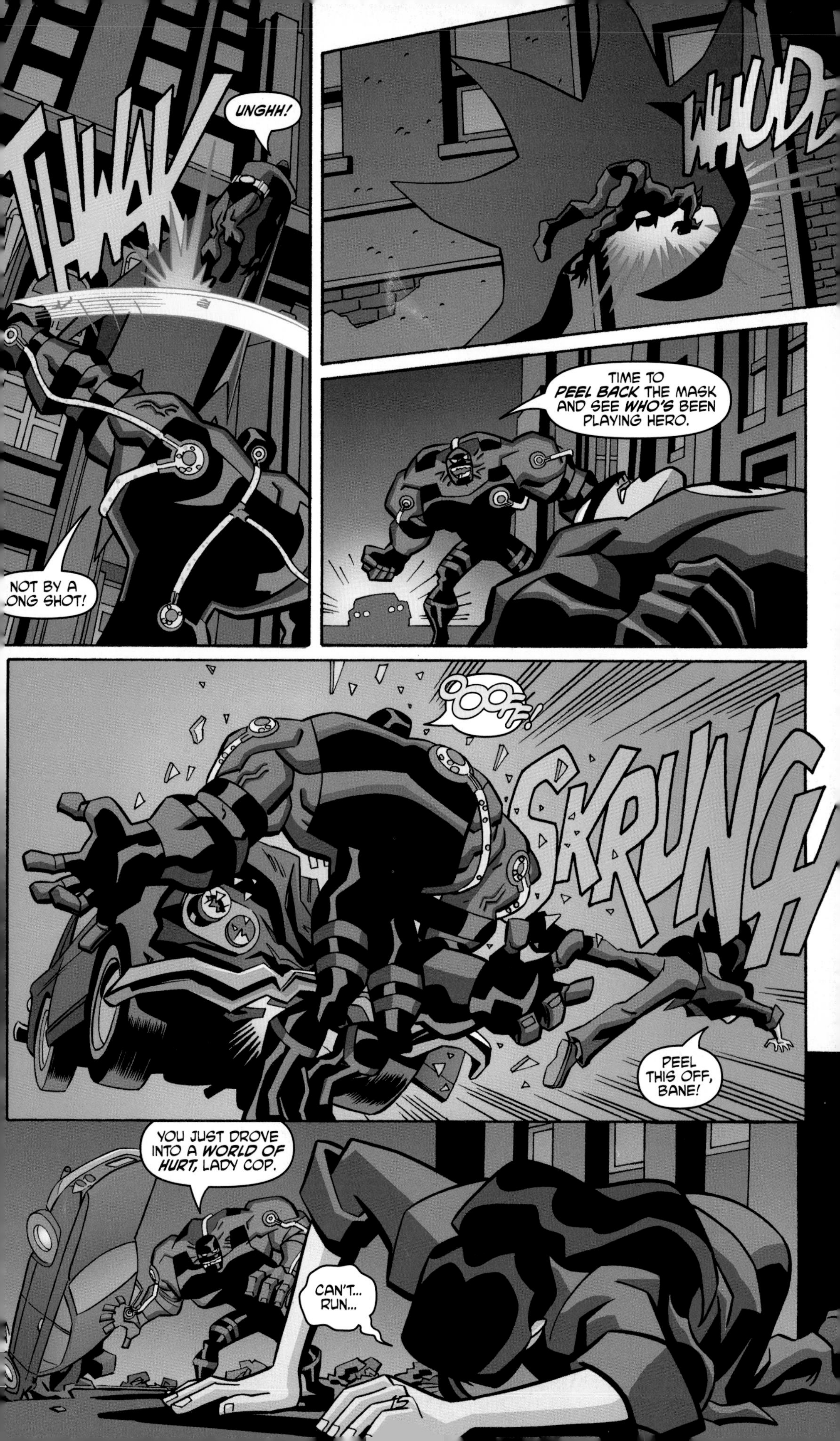
THWAK
UNGHH!
NOT BY A
LONG SHOT!
WHUDE
TIME TO PEEL BACK THE MASK AND SEE WHO'S BEEN PLAYING HERO.
OOOF!
SKRUNCH
PEEL THIS OFF, BANE!
YOU JUST DROVE INTO A WORLD OF HURT, LADY COP.
CAN'T... RUN...

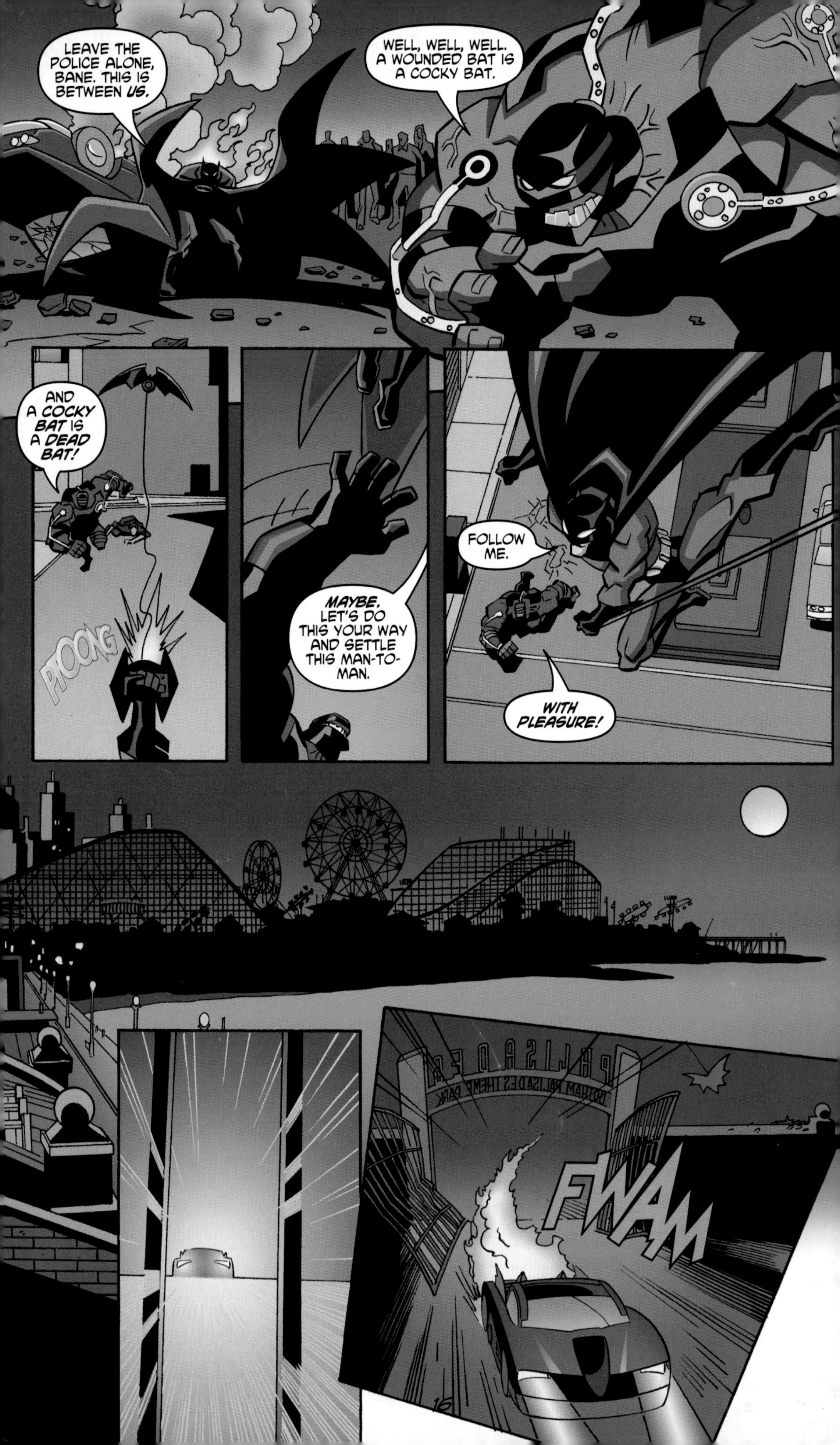

LEAVE THE POLICE ALONE, BANE. THIS IS BETWEEN *US.*
WELL, WELL, WELL. A WOUNDED BAT IS A COCKY BAT.
AND A *COCKY BAT* IS A *DEAD BAT!*
PTOONG
MAYBE. LET'S DO THIS YOUR WAY AND SETTLE THIS MAN-TO-MAN.
FOLLOW ME.
WITH PLEASURE!
FWAM

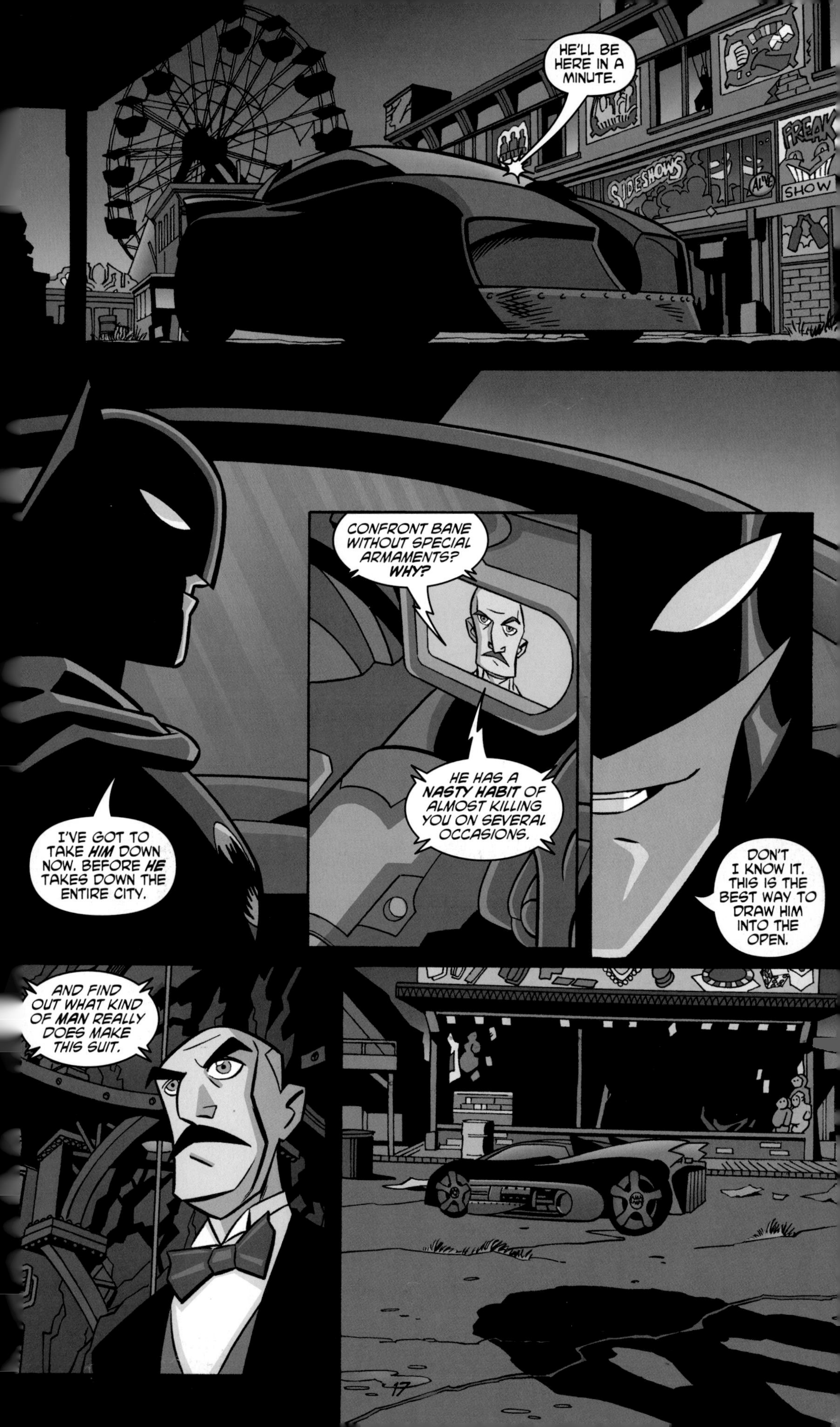

HE'LL BE HERE IN A MINUTE.
SIDESHOWS
ALIVE
FREAK SHOW
I'VE GOT TO TAKE HIM DOWN NOW. BEFORE HE TAKES DOWN THE ENTIRE CITY.
CONFRONT BANE WITHOUT SPECIAL ARMAMENTS? WHY?
HE HAS A NASTY HABIT OF ALMOST KILLING YOU ON SEVERAL OCCASIONS.
DON'T I KNOW IT. THIS IS THE BEST WAY TO DRAW HIM INTO THE OPEN.
AND FIND OUT WHAT KIND OF MAN REALLY DOES MAKE THIS SUIT.

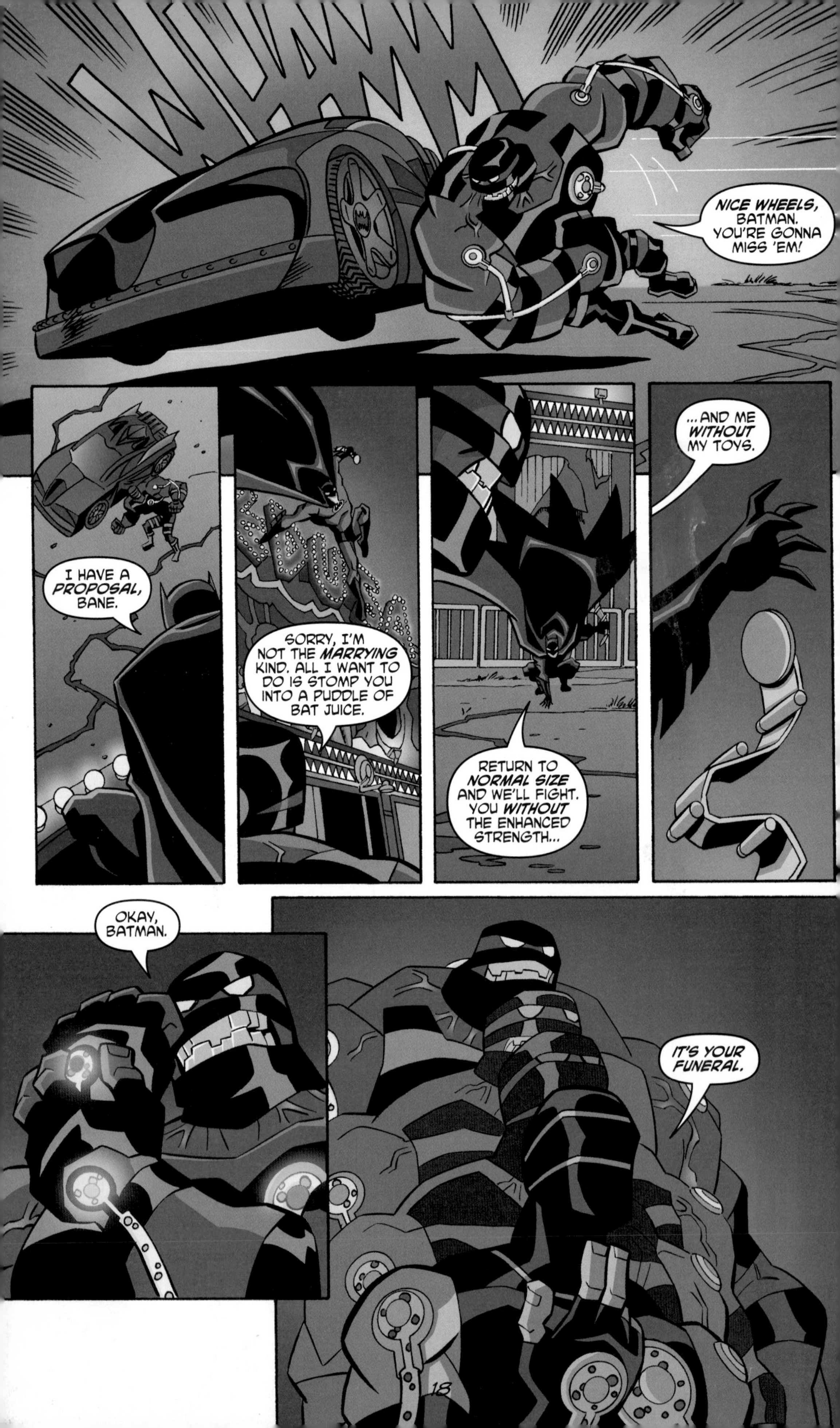
WHAMM
NICE WHEELS, BATMAN. YOU'RE GONNA MISS 'EM!
I HAVE A PROPOSAL, BANE.
SORRY, I'M NOT THE MARRYING KIND. ALL I WANT TO DO IS STOMP YOU INTO A PUDDLE OF BAT JUICE.
RETURN TO NORMAL SIZE AND WE'LL FIGHT. YOU WITHOUT THE ENHANCED STRENGTH...
...AND ME WITHOUT MY TOYS.
OKAY, BATMAN.
IT'S YOUR FUNERAL.

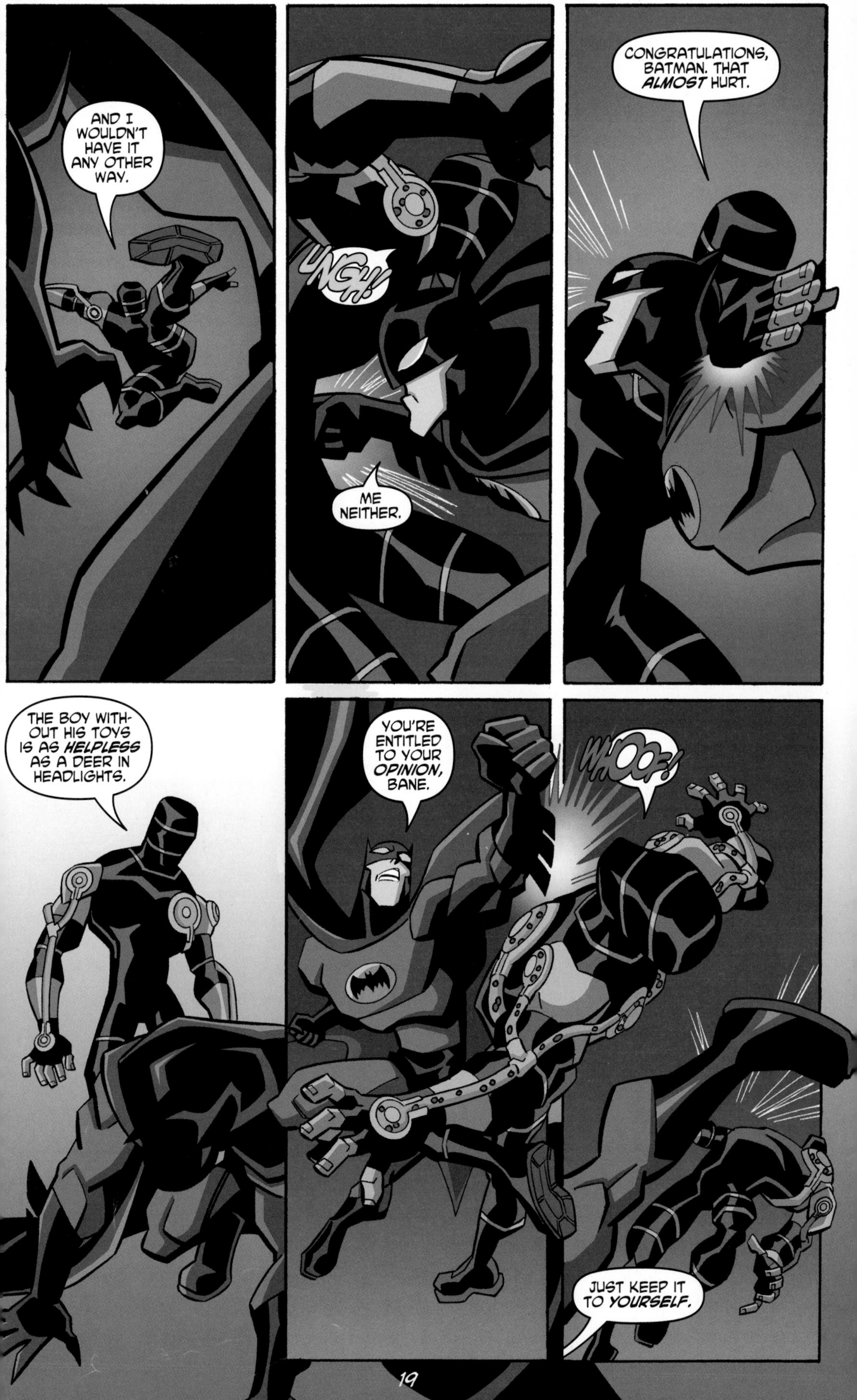
AND I WOULDN'T HAVE IT ANY OTHER WAY.
UNGH!
ME NEITHER.
CONGRATULATIONS, BATMAN. THAT ALMOST HURT.
THE BOY WITH-OUT HIS TOYS IS AS HELPLESS AS A DEER IN HEADLIGHTS.
YOU'RE ENTITLED TO YOUR OPINION, BANE.
WHOOF!
JUST KEEP IT TO YOURSELF.

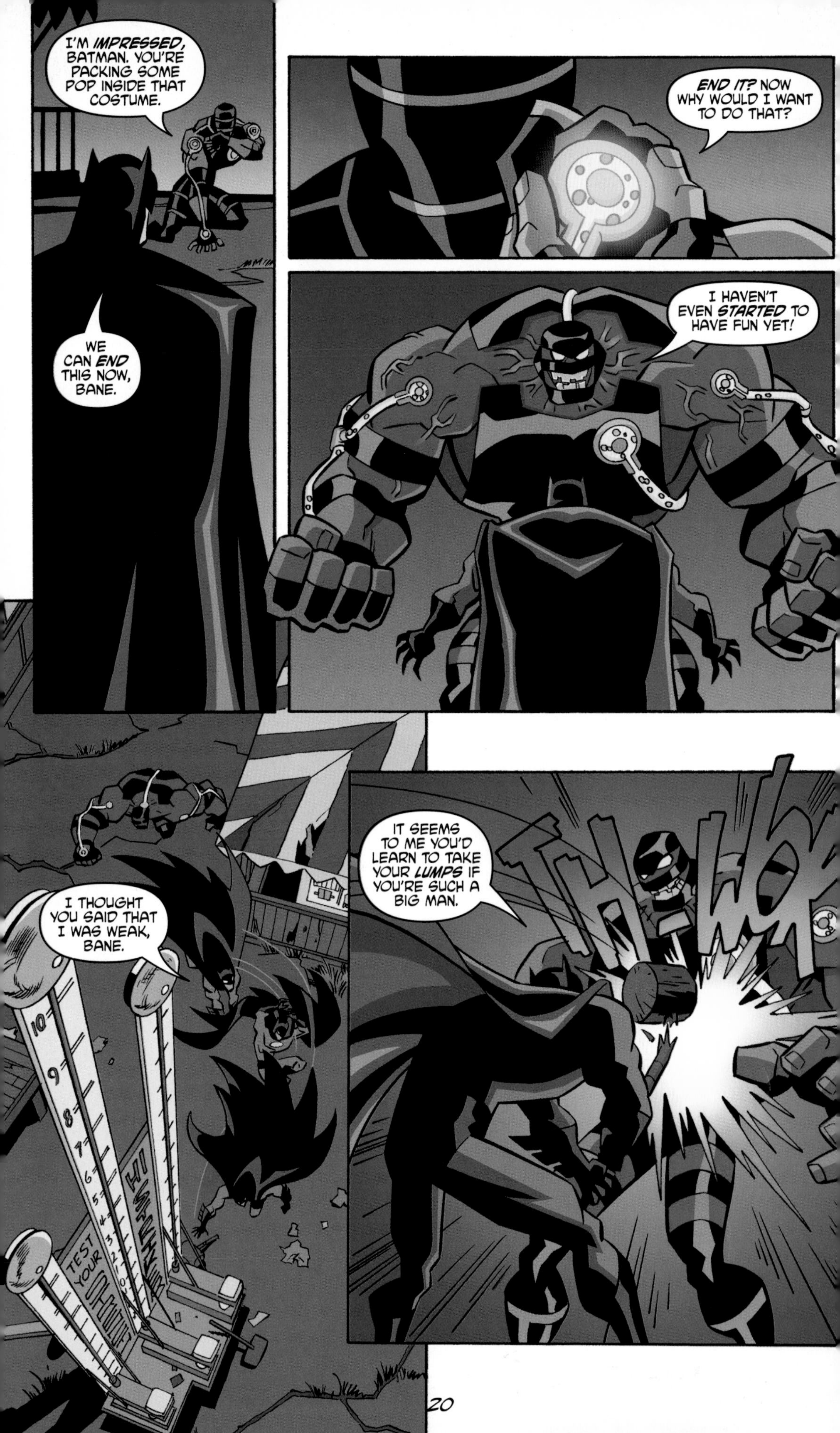
I'M IMPRESSED, BATMAN. YOU'RE PACKING SOME POP INSIDE THAT COSTUME.
WE CAN END THIS NOW, BANE.
END IT? NOW WHY WOULD I WANT TO DO THAT?
I HAVEN'T EVEN STARTED TO HAVE FUN YET!
I THOUGHT YOU SAID THAT I WAS WEAK, BANE.
TEST YOUR
IT SEEMS TO ME YOU'D LEARN TO TAKE YOUR LUMPS IF YOU'RE SUCH A BIG MAN.

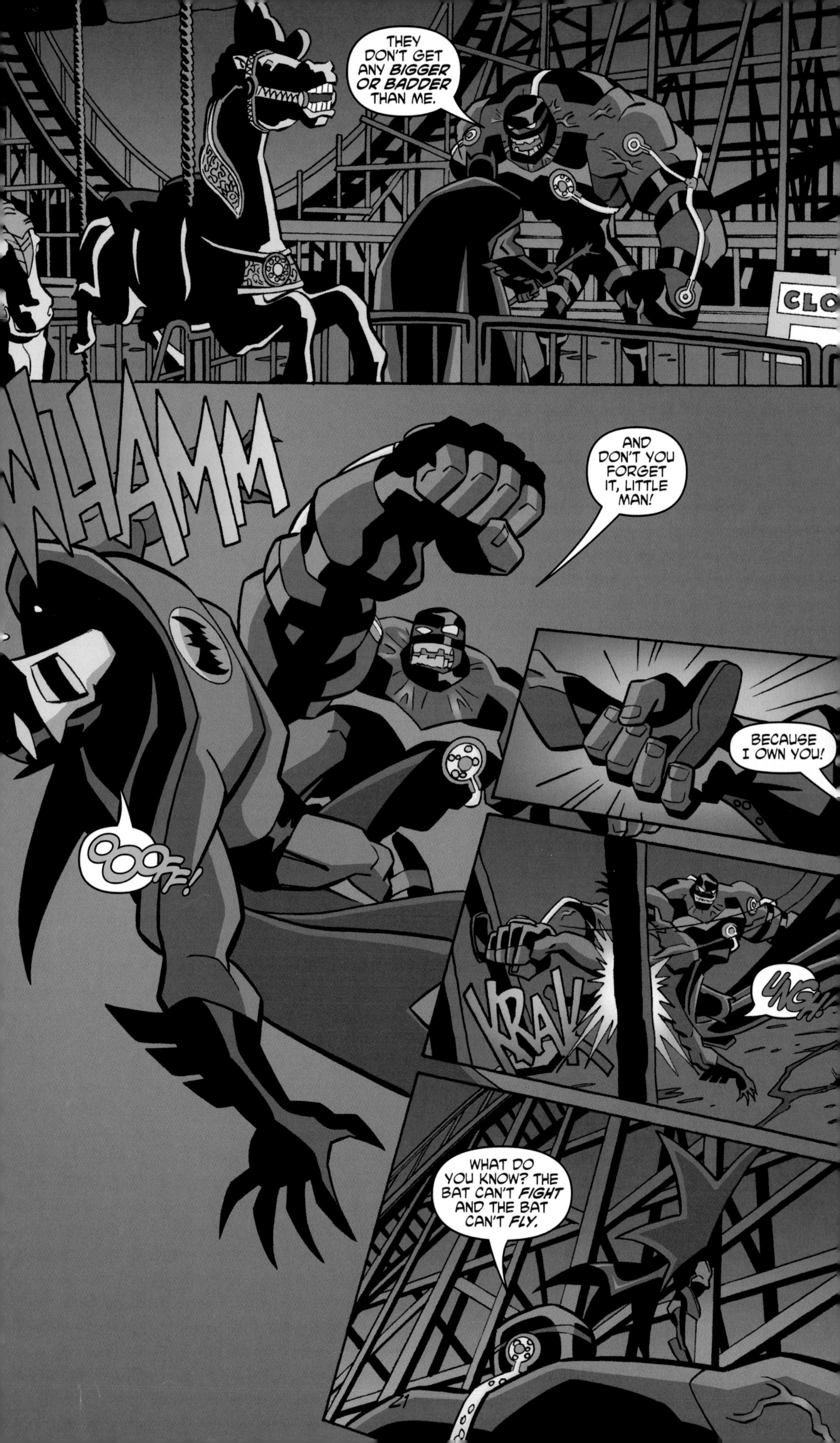
THEY DON'T GET ANY BIGGER OR BADDER THAN ME.
CLO
WHAMM
AND DON'T YOU FORGET IT, LITTLE MAN!
OOOFF!
BECAUSE I OWN YOU!
KRAK
UNGH!
WHAT DO YOU KNOW? THE BAT CAN'T FIGHT AND THE BAT CAN'T FLY.

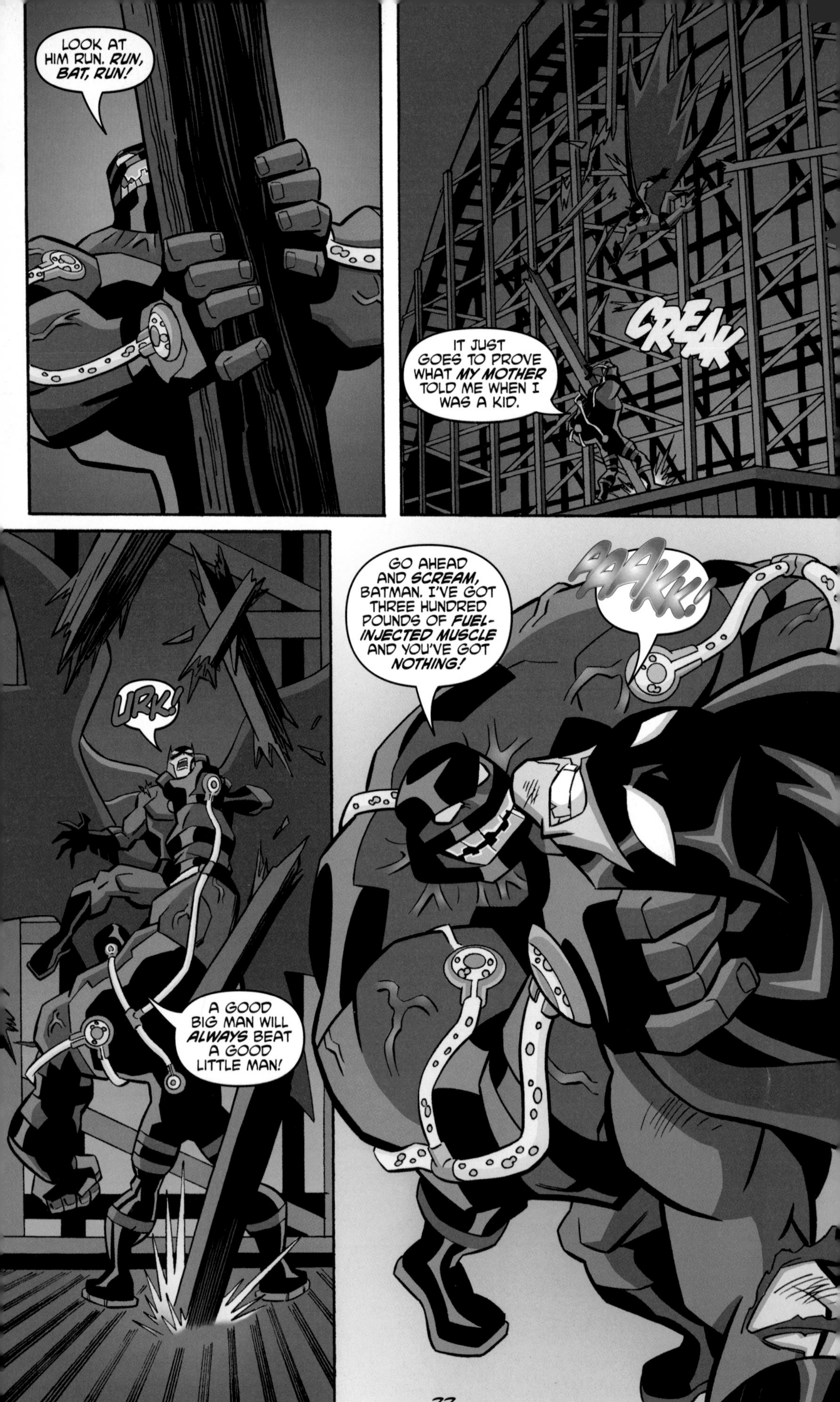
LOOK AT HIM RUN. RUN, BAT, RUN!
CREAK
IT JUST GOES TO PROVE WHAT MY MOTHER TOLD ME WHEN I WAS A KID.
URK!
A GOOD BIG MAN WILL ALWAYS BEAT A GOOD LITTLE MAN!
GO AHEAD AND SCREAM, BATMAN. I'VE GOT THREE HUNDRED POUNDS OF FUEL-INJECTED MUSCLE AND YOU'VE GOT NOTHING!
AAAKK!

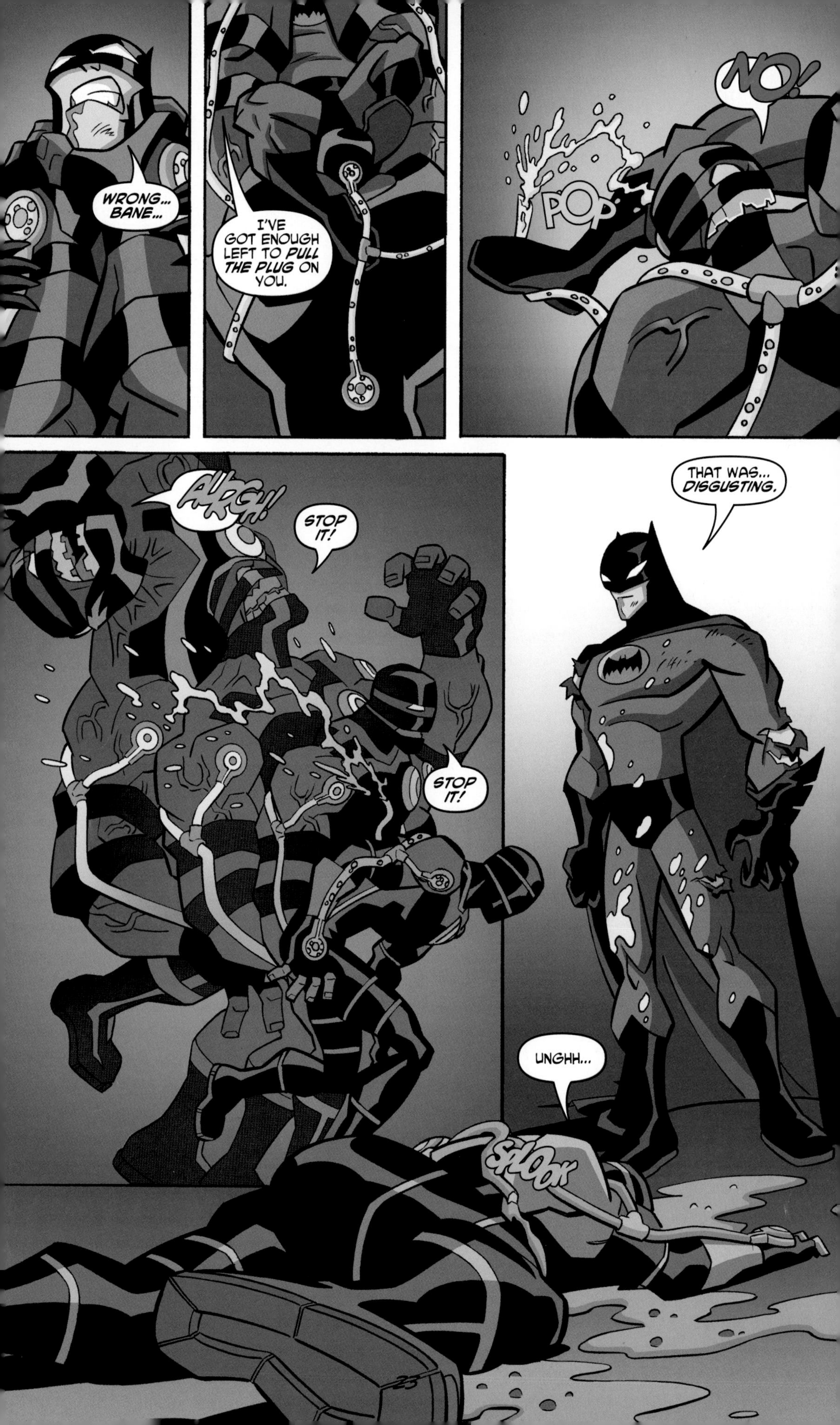
WRONG... BANE...
I'VE GOT ENOUGH LEFT TO PULL THE PLUG ON YOU.
POP
NO!
AURGH!
STOP IT!
STOP IT!
THAT WAS... DISGUSTING.
UNGHH...
SPLOOK

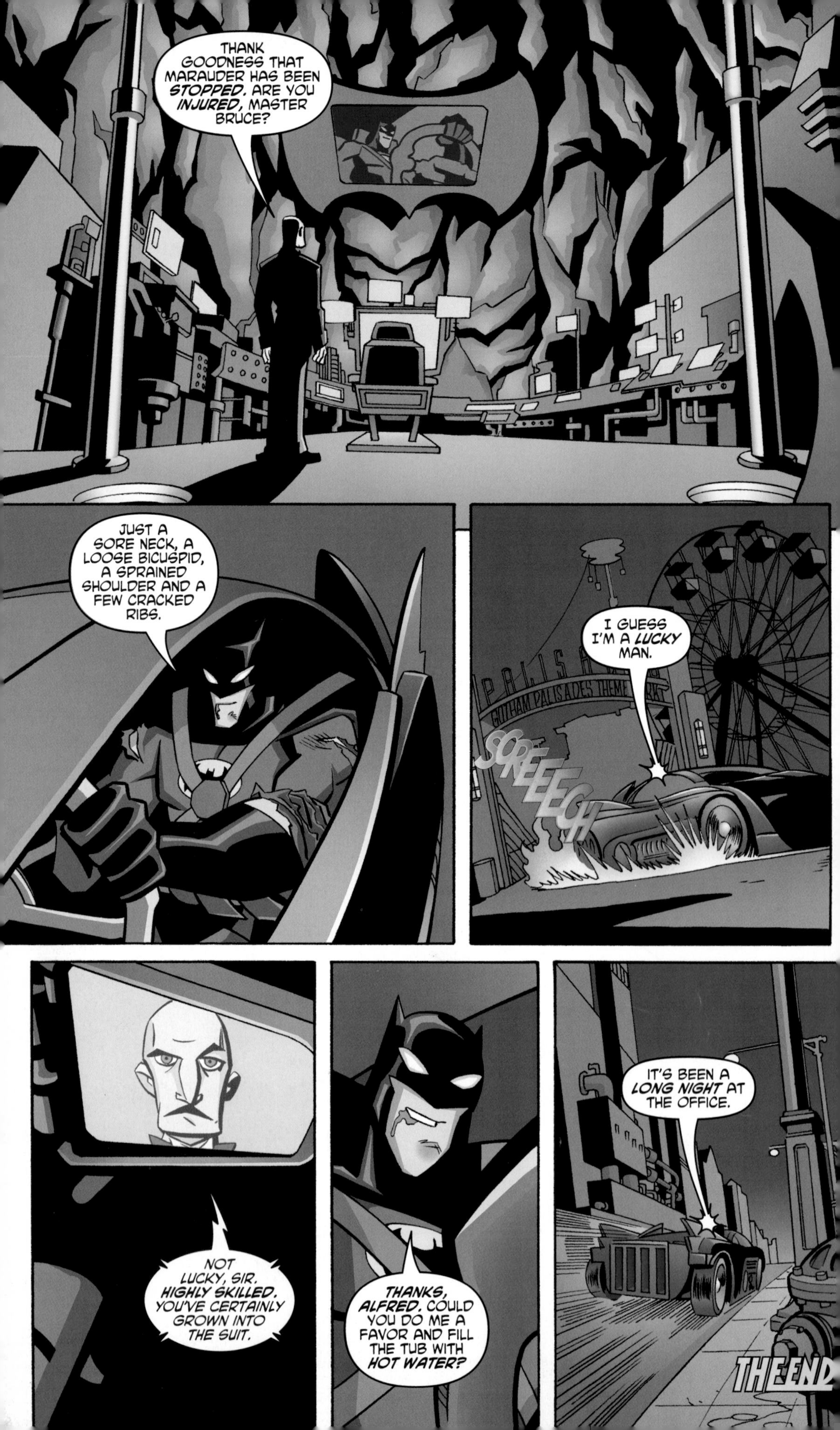
THANK GOODNESS THAT MARAUDER HAS BEEN STOPPED. ARE YOU INJURED, MASTER BRUCE?
JUST A SORE NECK, A LOOSE BICUSPID, A SPRAINED SHOULDER AND A FEW CRACKED RIBS.
I GUESS I'M A LUCKY MAN.
SCREEECH
NOT LUCKY, SIR. HIGHLY SKILLED. YOU'VE CERTAINLY GROWN INTO THE SUIT.
THANKS, ALFRED. COULD YOU DO ME A FAVOR AND FILL THE TUB WITH HOT WATER?
IT'S BEEN A LONG NIGHT AT THE OFFICE.
THE END

CREATORS

BILL MATHENY WRITER

Along with comics like THE BATMAN STRIKES, Bill Matheny has written for TV series including KRYPTO THE SUPERDOG, WHERE'S WALDO, A PUP NAMED SCOOBY-DOO, and many others.

CHRISTOPHER JONES PENCILLER

Christopher Jones is an artist that has worked for DC Comics, Image, Malibu, Caliber, and Sundragon Comics.

TERRY BEATTY INKER

Terry Beatty has inked THE BATMAN STRIKES! and BATMAN: THE BRAVE AND THE BOLD as well as several other DC Comics graphic novels.

GLOSSARY

armaments (AR-muh-ments)--weapons and other equipment used for fighting battles

arsenal (AR-suh-nuhl)--a place where weapons and ammunition are made or stored

batarang (BAT-uh-rang)--a projectile-like weapon that Batman uses that is similar to a boomerang

cocky (KOK-ee)--arrogant or overconfident

confront (kuhn-FRUHNT)--to come face to face with something, or to meet someone in a threatening or accusing way

disgusting (diss-GUHSS-ting)--very unpleasant and offensive to others

enhanced (en-HANSSD)--better or greater

entitled (en-TYE-tuhld)--gave a right or a privilege to someone

marauder (muh-ROD-ur)--an invader or attacker

payback (PAY-bak)--revenge

proposal (pruh-POSE-uhl)--a plan or idea

regulates (REG-yuh-lates)--controls, manages, or adjusts

vital (VYE-tuhl)--very important, or having to do with life, like vital signs

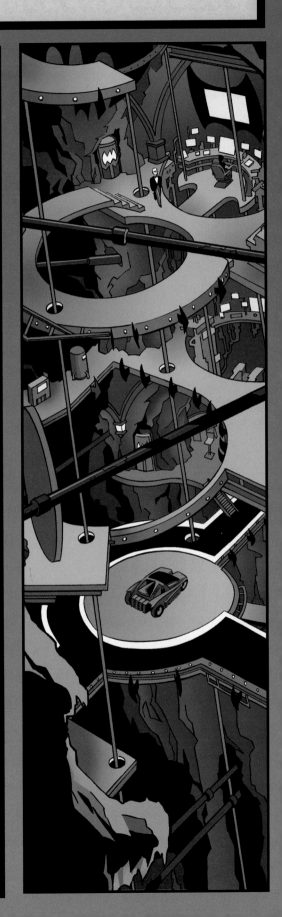

VISUAL QUESTIONS & PROMPTS

1. The artists show Bane transforming into his normal form by using transparent, overlapped images. What are some others ways they could've shown him transform?

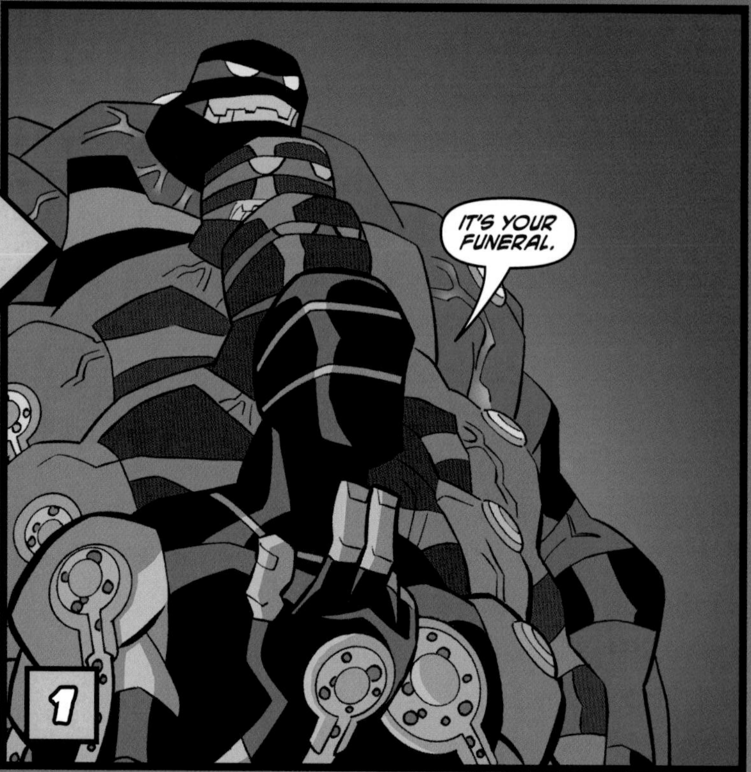

1
IT'S YOUR FUNERAL.

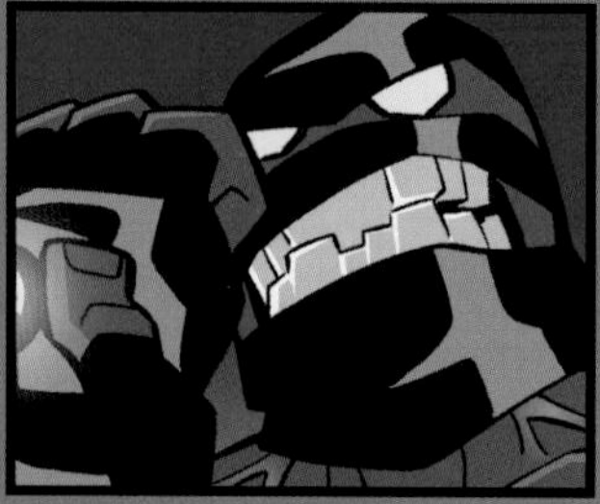

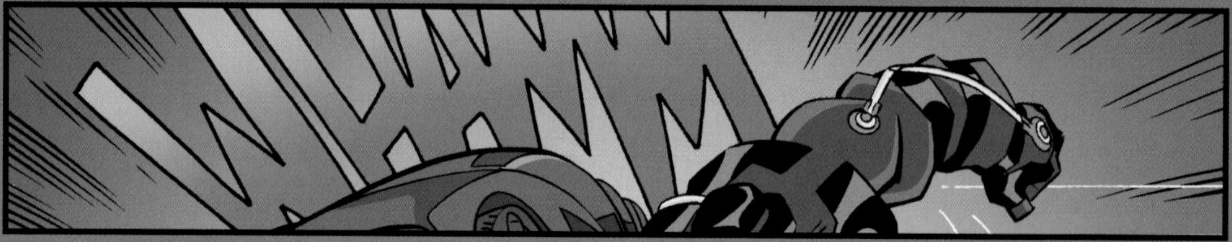

2. Why do you think Alfred wishes Batman would let him know before using the remote to activate the Batmobile?

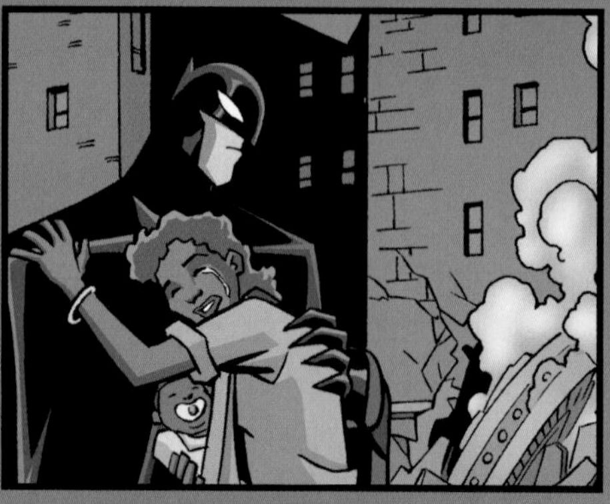

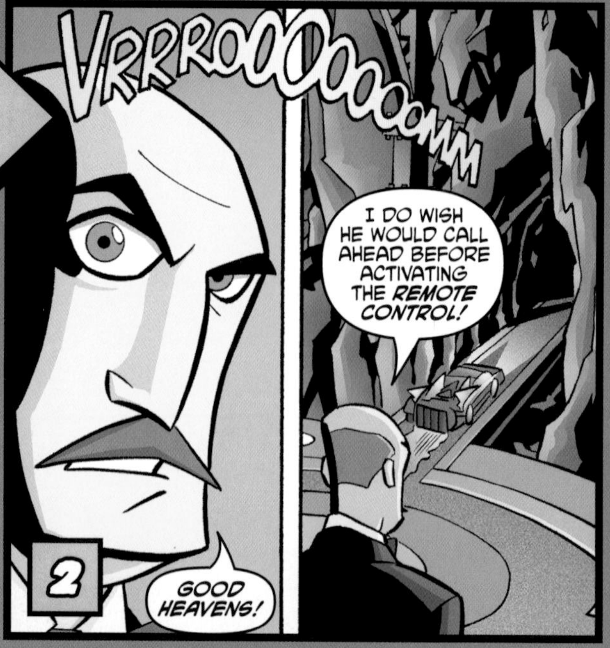

VRRROOOOOOOOMM
I DO WISH HE WOULD CALL AHEAD BEFORE ACTIVATING THE *REMOTE CONTROL!*
2
GOOD HEAVENS!

3. Bane's power comes from a chemical called Venom that makes him super-strong. If you were super-strong, what would you use your newfound strength to do? Why?

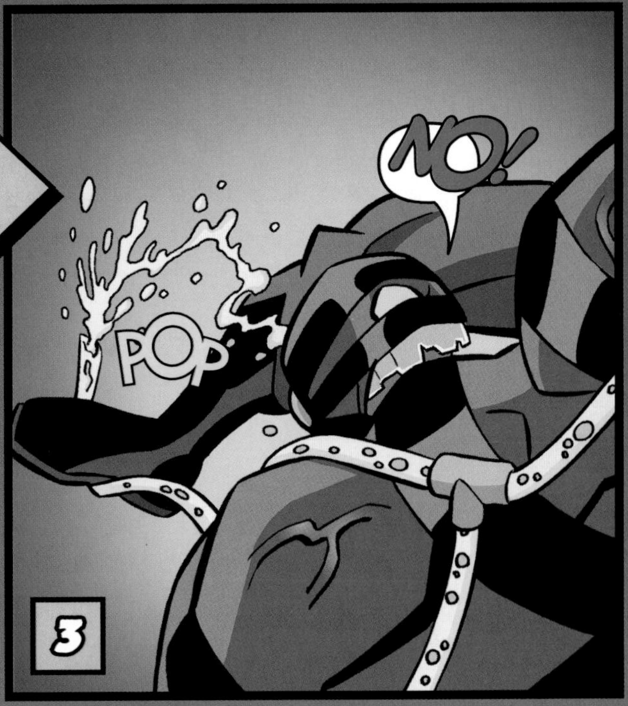
NO!
POP
3

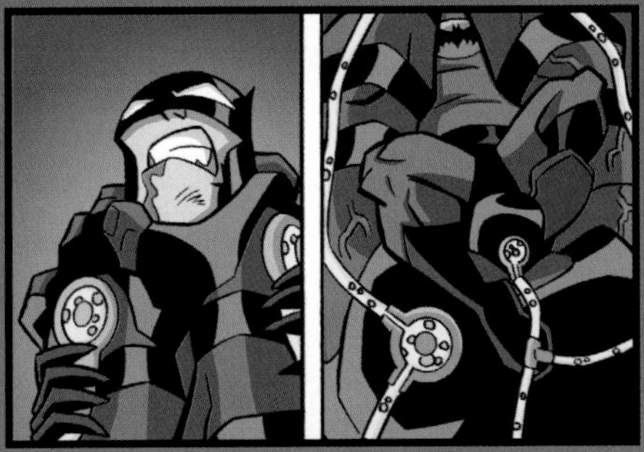

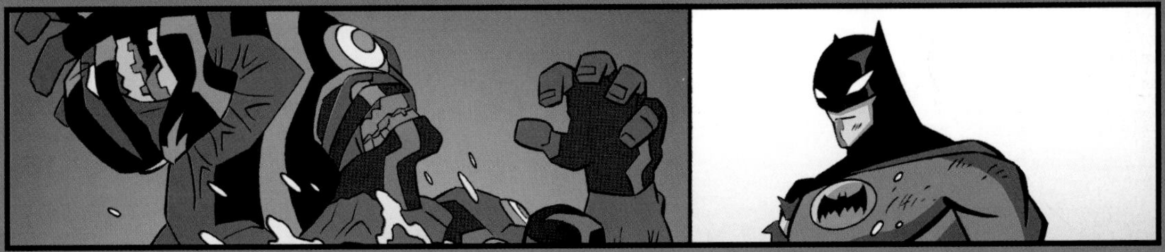

4. At one point in this story, Batman drops his Utility Belt. What skills and abilities could Batman use to fight crime without his tools and gadgets?

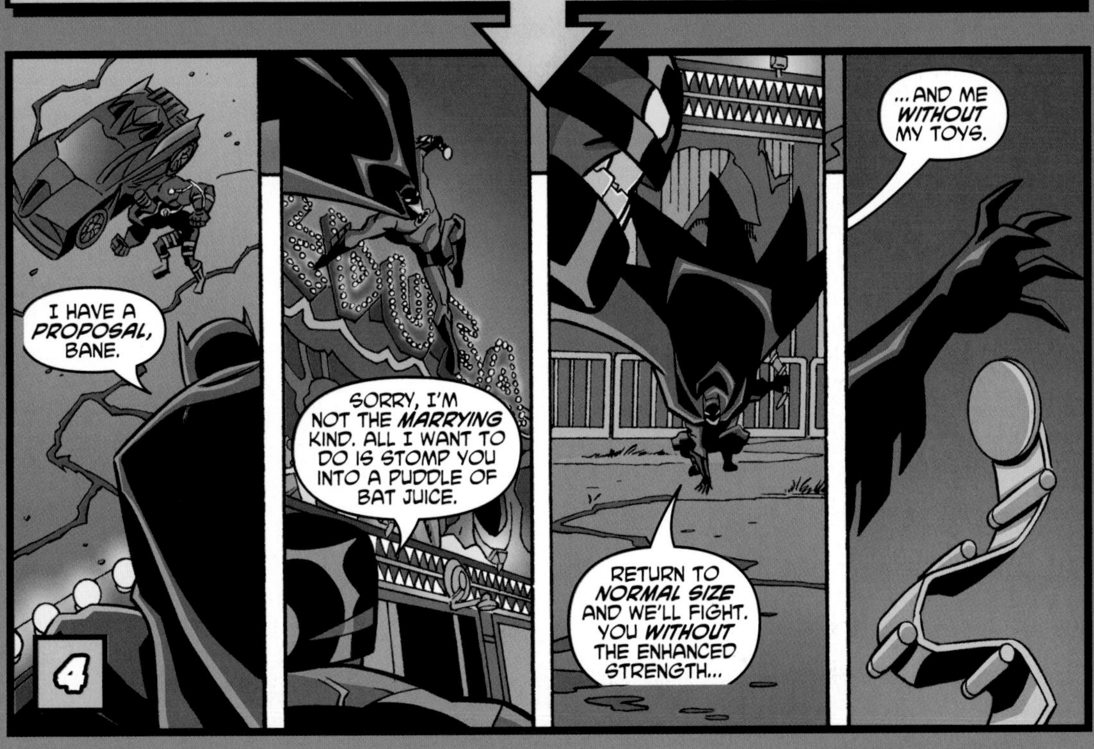
I HAVE A *PROPOSAL,* BANE.
SORRY, I'M NOT THE *MARRYING* KIND. ALL I WANT TO DO IS STOMP YOU INTO A PUDDLE OF BAT JUICE.
RETURN TO *NORMAL SIZE* AND WE'LL FIGHT. YOU *WITHOUT* THE ENHANCED STRENGTH...
...AND ME *WITHOUT* MY TOYS.
4

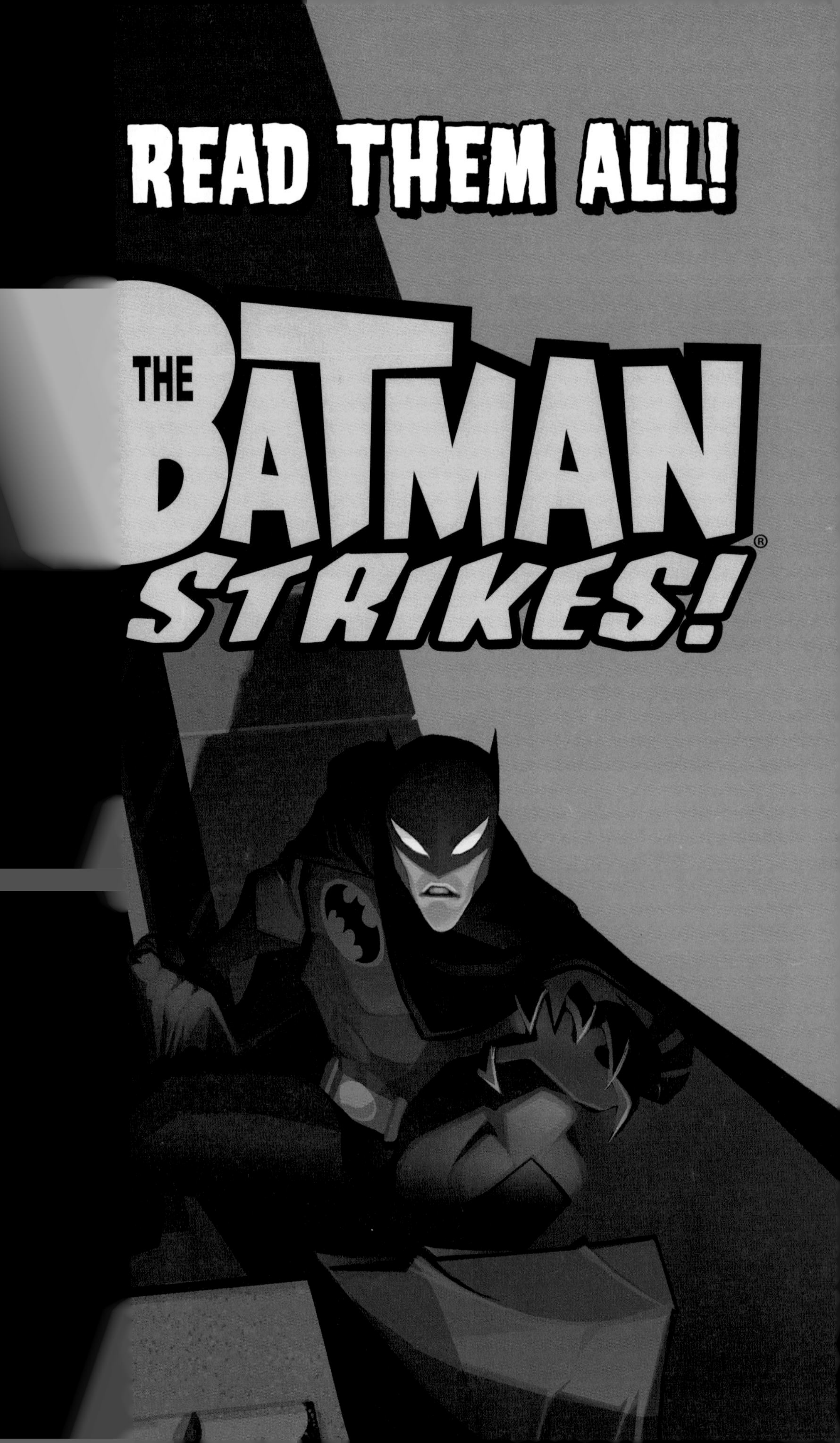
READ THEM ALL!
THE BATMAN STRIKES!

DC COMICS
THE BATMAN STRIKES!
IN THE CLUTCHES OF THE PENGUIN!
MATHENY · JONES · BEATTY

DC COMICS
THE BATMAN STRIKES!
BANE ON THE RAMPAGE!
MATHENY · JONES · BEATTY

DC COMICS
THE BATMAN STRIKES!
GOING... BATTY!
MATHENY · JONES · BEATTY

DC COMICS
THE BATMAN STRIKES!
Joker's Wild!
MATHENY
JONES
BEATTY

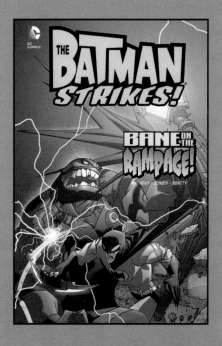

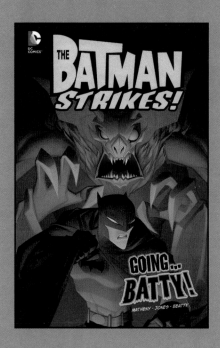

THE BATMAN® STRIKES!

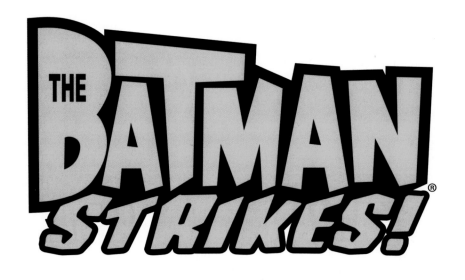